The Reluctant Dog

Written
by Dina Wills

Illustrated
by Jeff Byrd

ISBN: 9780615451954
ISBN 13: 0615451950

For Michael

Lily LaRou was having a bad day,
which, oddly enough, began the usual way.

She was under a tree with a curious bee,
pondering the day and serving tea.

The strange little frown on her face didn't fit.
It didn't belong, not one little bit.

Suddenly she said, "I can't pretend anymore.
I'm feeling lonely, and this party's a bore.

I need a real friend who'll always care.
And I know where to go and how to get there."

So the next morning she left with a yawn,
to find a best friend not long after dawn.

She passed the post office, the corner store, too,
then a few minutes later she passed by the zoo.

Although uncertain about what she would find,
she knew her friend would be one of a kind.

She wanted to teach him to sit, shake, and stay.
And then, of course, she wanted to play.

Far Far Away was at the end of a road.
It was dusty and bumpy and home to a big toad.

"There you are, dear," he said. "You're late!
Just follow the path right up to the gate."

"The dogs born here are royalty, it's told.
Their father's a prince and a sight to behold."

"You were expecting me?" she asked, confused.
"Indeed I was," he said, somewhat amused.

Inside was chaos, but one dog was cool,
so cool in fact, he was oozing drool.

Most of the others were clowning around.
They were bouncing and pouncing all over the ground.

It was very clear they were trying to impress,
but clearer still *he* couldn't care less.

Lily fell in love with this cute little guy,
then she named him Cole, though, it's unclear why.

Now boys and girls, be careful what you wish for. . .

Cole wasn't the kind of dog you could simply ignore.

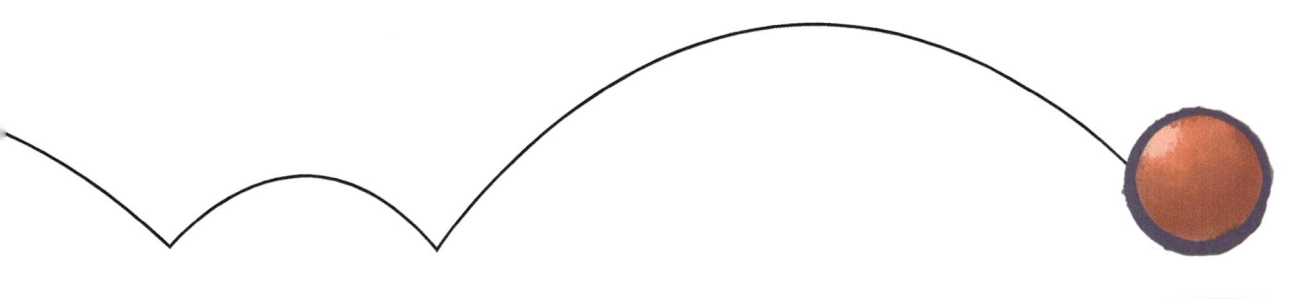

It didn't take long for Lily to find out,
that being a dog wasn't what he was about!

He didn't want to fetch anything at all,
not a toy, not a stick, not even a ball.

He simply refused to sit, shake, or stay.
And weirder still, he refused to play.

Lily would say, "Come!" and he would sit.
So after a while, she finally quit.

He didn't behave
like most dogs do.
But worst of all,
he was difficult, too!

She built him a house
fit for a king.
But he wasn't impressed.
He hated the thing.

He expected breakfast
each morning at six.
But if Lily slept in,
he had a few tricks.

Taking him for a walk was a big ordeal,
because try as she might, he refused to heel.

Lily loved to canoe on Dancing Bear Lake,
but had to stop going for everyone's sake.

And then the unthinkable happened one day.
Cole jumped the fence, refusing to stay!

He caused such a scene in front of her school,
that she sank in her chair and felt like a fool.

"Boy, please!" Lily said, getting down on one knee.
"You're a dog, not a prince. Why won't you mind me?"

He stared back at her with wise, unblinking eyes.
And then she understood. . . Cole was in disguise.

He looked like a dog
on the outside, it's true.
But inside his head,
he had a different view.

So the remedy was simple.
She knew what to do.
From that day forward
she followed his cue.

Taking him for a walk
was no longer an ordeal.
She gave him the leash
and walked at his heel.

He rode in the canoe
on Dancing Bear Lake,
which caused quite a scene,
and a few double takes.

She took him to school so he wasn't alone,
and they gave him a chair that resembled a throne.

Lily dubbed him Sir Cole, of Far Far Away,
then the toad winked at him and shouted, "Hooray!"

They lived happily ever after, after that.

Lily never ever had another bad day.
And Cole, well he finally did . . .

learn how to play.

www.ingramcontent.com/pod-product-compliance
Lightning Source LLC
Chambersburg PA
CBHW041557120626
46551CB00002B/239